Max opened his mouth to speak, but his tongue suddenly felt five sizes too big and all he could manage was a mumble.

'Are you OK?' asked Molly. 'You're all sweaty.'

Max shook his head and clutched his sides. They were aching sharply, like they were about to split wide open!

His skin itched, as thick wiry hairs began to push through his pores. Four big bumps bulged out from his ribs, doubling him over in pain. They stretched and grew until they were as long as his arms.

'M-Molly,' Max managed. He looked up and saw he was less than half the height of his sister. 'I can't miss this lesson!'

Molly watched in amazement as six extra eyes sprouted on her brother's forehead. They blinked at her, one after the other.

One school holiday, Max and Molly go with their zoologist parents to Africa. Max develops a strange fever when he drinks from a stream and, after he's recovered, everything has changed – especially his attitude to animals.

The village healer tells him he now has a special skill: he's at one with the animals. But Max doesn't believe a word of it. At least, not until the first time his fingers tingle, his vision goes wobbly and his tongue gets thick and fuzzy ...

Luckily, the effects never last more than a few hours, but that's still plenty of time for Max to get into some amazing scrapes, and to get first-hand experience of how the animal world sees humans.

For a boy who wants nothing more challenging than a computer game and a chocolate bar, life just got a whole lot more complicated ...

Illustrations by Brian Williamson

EGMONT

Special thanks to:
Barry Hutchison, West Jesmond Primary School,
Maney Hill Primary School
and Courthouse Junior School

EGMONT
We bring stories to life

Spider Swat first published in Great Britain 2008
by Egmont UK Limited
239 Kensington High Street, London W8 6SA

Text & illustrations © 2008 Egmont UK Ltd
Text by Barry Hutchison
Illustrations by Brian Williamson

ISBN 978 1 4052 3939 4

1 3 5 7 9 10 8 6 4 2

A CIP catalogue record for this title is available
from the British Library

Typeset by Avon DataSet Ltd, Bidford on Avon, Warwickshire
Printed and bound in Great Britain by the CPI Group

BEASTLY!: The Characters

MAX MURPHY From two eyes to eight in the blink of . . . well, an eye!

Absent-minded Uncle Herbert looks after Max and his twin sister Molly during term time while their parents are away.

MOLLY MURPHY
A sisterly sidekick well trained in keeping secrets

Max longs for a normal family life, but that's about as likely as his uncle remembering which day of the week it is!

HERBERT SPLOTT
Sometimes he seems to have lost the plot

BEASTLY!: The Characters

Mr and Mrs Murphy are zoologists, so they're completely crazy about animals, and they're busy working on creating the best animal encyclopedia ever. Max thinks they're weird; who wants to stand around staring at sloths when you could be tucked up at home watching telly?

MR MURPHY AND MRS MURPHY
They don't realise their son's on the web – and not the Internet kind!

PROFESSOR SLYNK
Good with electronics –
not so good on a treadmill!

And, as if all that didn't make Max's life tough enough, his parents' sinister colleague Professor Preston Slynk has found out his secret. Slynk's miniature insect-robot spies are never far away . . .

SPIDERS: The Facts

They're a variety pack!
There are over 30,000 species of spider.

They don't leave waste!
Most spiders make a new web every day. They don't waste the old one though – they roll it into a ball and gobble it up!

They're super big!
Tarantulas are the biggest of all spiders (one type – the South American bird spider is around 25 centimetres! – and can live for up to 30 years!

They lay lots of eggs!
A female tarantula can lay anything from 500 to 1000 eggs at one time!

They bite! Only the Australian funnel web spiders are to be avoided, but with only two registered bites a year, they're nothing to worry about.

They're scary! A fear of spiders is known as *arachnophobia*. It is one of the most common phobias in humans.

ENGLAND: The Facts

- The population of England is around 50 million – roughly 10 times as many people as lived there in England in Tudor times

- Between 1066 and 1362, the official language of England was ... French!

- The capital, London, is the largest city in Europe

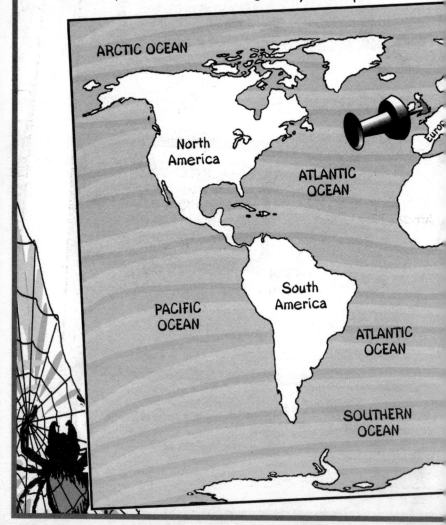

- On 10 August 2003, a temperature of 38.5 degrees Celsius was recorded in Brogdale, Kent - the highest recorded temperature in England to date
- The biggest spider found in England is the raft spider, with a leg span of 7 centimetres - not too small to stop your sister from screaming, but just small enough for your mum to trap it under a glass!

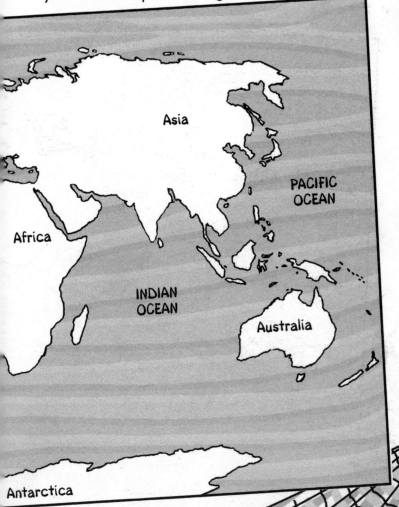

Contents

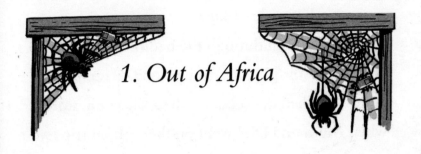

1. Out of Africa

'Breakfast special!' Uncle Herbert yelled up the stairs. 'Come and get it!'

'Oh, no,' groaned Max, hiding under his quilt. 'That's all I need.'

Molly knocked on his bedroom door, 'Hurry up, Max. It might be something interesting.'

'I'd just like something normal,' he muttered, then shouted. 'I'll be down in five minutes.' He crawled out of bed and started his morning routine:

- Stare blearily into the mirror and pat down cockatoo-like tufts of hair
- Clear a path through the bedroom by pushing yesterday's dirty plates, mugs and crisp packets under the bed (adding to the collection started when Mum and Dad went on their Africa trip two weeks ago)
- Rummage through the jumble on the floor and rescue all socks
- Yawn like a hippo while putting on the freshest socks from the pile
- Repeat as above for pants, shirt and trousers
- Search under bed for games console and through jumble of clothes for last week's history homework – due in yesterday!
- Empty sweet wrappers and comics from school bag. Cram crumpled history homework (plus fresh supply of crisps and chocolate biscuits) into bag

• Drag bag downstairs and dump it in the middle of the hall

• Shuffle into the kitchen and collapse, exhausted, on to a chair

With Mum and Dad away, making breakfast was the job of Uncle Herbert, whose taste buds came from a charity shop on Planet Weird. Last week he had served up chicken drumsticks in custard, mackerel and trifle pie, and then strawberry tikka masala with gravy.

'D'you mind if I just have cereal today, Uncle Herbert?' asked Max.

'If you like, Max. Before you decide, however, I should mention that I've made my "Monday Special", so you may change your mind.'

'Really?' said Max suspiciously. 'What's that?'

'Guess!' teased his uncle. 'Here's a clue: put the darkest thing next to water with an "a" not an "e", add a fish – but not a red one – and cook in a case.'

'That's easy!' said Molly, who'd seen the empty packets in the bin . . . and chosen cornflakes. 'Come on, Max.'

Max stared at the ceiling for a while, then said, 'I'm really sorry, Uncle Herbert, but I can't think. I've got two zillion tests coming up and I can't concentrate on anything else.'

'Except playing very important computer games all night,' snorted Molly.

'But that's for relaxation, *after* I've done my revision!'

Uncle Herbert started whistling and Max looked up, pleased to change the subject. 'Is that a clue?'

Still whistling, Uncle Herbert nodded.

'Um . . . song . . . long . . . spaghetti?' suggested Max.

Uncle Herbert shook his head.

'Song . . . tune . . . tuna! Something with tuna?'

'No!' said Molly, as Uncle Herbert mimed

switching off the light, then digging a hole. 'The whistling was a red herring – get it?'

'Switch ... itch ... pepper?'

Again, Uncle Herbert shook his head.

'Light ... delight ... Turkish delight?'

'Pathetic!' said Molly. 'It's sooo simple. The darkest thing is black. Put it next to water with an "e" not an "a" equals *blackcurrant*. Add a fish – but not a red one – is *herring*. Cook in a case equals *pie. So,* it's blackcurrant and herring pie, isn't it, Uncle?' Molly preened herself.

'Well done, Molly!' smiled Uncle Herbert tucking into a large bowlful. 'Mmm, this is good! Help yourself, Max.'

'Er . . . I'm not very hungry this morning,' said Max. 'I think I'll just have cornflakes.'

As Max poured his milk the doorbell rang. Uncle Herbert left the table to answer it.

'Molly,' whispered Max. 'I *really* need some help. Can you do my English essay for me? It's just that I've got all these tests coming up and I've got behind with my French, history and science.'

Molly folded her arms and tilted her head, just like Mum. 'Is that all?'

'Oh, yes. I forgot. Maths.'

'And . . .?'

'And geography.'

'Have you noticed,' said Molly, 'that, being the same age –'

'*Nearly* the same age,' said Max. 'I'm ten

minutes older, remember?'

Molly ignored the taunt. 'As I was saying, being the same age, we both get exactly the same work. So how come I'm bang up to date and you're so . . . useless?'

'I am *not*!'

Molly raised her eyebrows. 'Computer games. Need I say more?'

'It's not my fault. It's the games companies. They keep bringing out new levels. If I stopped playing I'd lose my ranking.'

'I do your homework so you can play games? I don't think so. There's an easy answer – concentrate on your schoolwork.'

'You sound just like Mum. Anyway, it's not the games. It's the animal transformations. They keep happening and I can't stop thinking about it. Please help me, Molly. If you don't I'll do really badly in all the tests.

'OK,' said Molly. 'But only if you unplug that computer!'

Max was about to protest when the kitchen door shuddered and Uncle Herbert's voice mumbled from the other side, 'Ah, yes! Always a good idea to open it first.'

Then in came an enormous parcel covered in stickers that said, 'Fragile,' and 'This Way up'. It was followed into the room by Uncle Herbert.

'It's from Africa and addressed to you two,' he said. 'It must be from your Mum and Dad!' He dropped it on the floor and went back in the hall to sign the delivery slip.

The twins rushed over and ripped open the box. They started pulling out handfuls of straw padding and trying to guess what might be inside.

'Huh!' said Max, holding up a piece of bright red-and-yellow cloth. 'A tea towel? What's the point? I never do the drying up.'

'Maybe that *is* the point!' laughed Molly.

'This looks better,' he said picking up a small statue of a man with a tooth necklace and a sharp bone through his nose. It reminded him of the village healer he'd met the first time he'd transformed.

'This is cool,' he said. Then in a hopeful whisper he added, 'Hey, Molly. Do you think this might be to help me control the transformations?'

'No. How could it be? Mum and Dad don't know about them, do they?'

Max felt disappointed, but continued emptying the box. He looked at the growing pile of bead bracelets, shell necklaces and carved animals. There were even shakers like the maracas they had at primary school.

'This is all rubbish! Why on earth did Mum and Dad think we'd want this heap of junk?'

Molly reached to the bottom of the box. 'Hold

on! This looks interesting.'

'Oh, yeah?'

'No, really. Look!' said Molly, lifting out a face mask carved from dark rosewood. It had empty, cut-out eyes and real human teeth that stuck up like crooked tombstones. It was painted all over with white spots and red lines, and from the chin hung a beard made of animal hair.

'Wow! That's *scary*!' said Max.

'It's like the ones we've been studying in art. I'll

take it to school – maybe we could draw it in still life.'

'It'd be better than a boring bowl of fruit,' said Max.

Just as Molly shoved the mask into her bag Max saw one of the eyes move! *But it couldn't*, he thought. *They're just holes*. He stepped back, pointing at Molly's bag.

'Er . . . Molly. I think –' he began. Then the doorbell rang again suddenly.

'Your friend Jake's here,' called Uncle Herbert.

Max and Molly grabbed their bags and soon all three of them were chatting and walking up the road to school.

'What were you saying earlier, Max?' asked Molly as they turned the corner at the end of the road.

'Saying? When?'

'Just before Jake arrived.'

'Um . . . I don't remember,' said Max. 'It can't have been anything important.'

But inside Molly's bag something really was moving and it wasn't going to help Max's schoolwork at all.

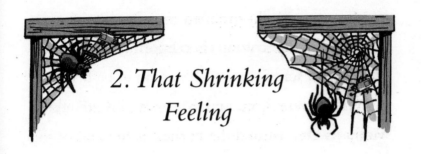

2. That Shrinking Feeling

'You're so lucky,' said Samreen, as she and Molly approached the school. 'A real tribal mask, all the way from Africa!'

'It is pretty impressive,' Molly admitted. 'Hand carved, too!'

Max and Jake trudged along behind the girls, pulling faces and rolling their eyes.

'Anyone can carve a mask,' Max sniffed. 'Once they start hand carving games consoles, then I'll be impressed.'

'We'll be doing our own carving today,' grinned Jake. The others looked at him, puzzled. 'Biology,' he explained. 'We're cutting up a frog!'

'Oh, yes,' said Samreen. 'It's going to be brilliant.'

'That's today?' gasped Max. 'Is this the thing we've got the test on later in the week?'

'This and last week's experiment,' Molly nodded. 'The one you . . . er . . . missed.'

Max and Molly were in different classes for most subjects, but luckily they had science lessons together and Jake and Molly had promised to come in early to help Max catch up on the work he'd missed.

'Where were you that day, anyway?' asked Samreen.

'I was . . . ill,' Max fibbed. He didn't like lying to his friends, but he couldn't tell Samreen he'd turned into a cat and spent the whole afternoon being chased by stray dogs!

'Do you think it'll burst open?' Jake asked, his eyes wide with excitement.

'Do we think what'll burst open?' frowned Molly.

'The frog! I heard they squirt guts everywhere when you cut into them!'

'Eew, that's disgusting!' laughed Samreen gleefully. 'But it's definitely true. I heard about one class where the blood squirted right across the room and into the teacher's eye! She smelled of frog guts for a month!'

Jake smiled as he pictured the gory scene.

'Cool!'

'Did I tell you what else was in the box?' interrupted Molly, changing the subject.

'No,' replied Samreen. 'What?'

'Wind chimes.'

'Hand carved?' Samreen gasped.

'Of course!'

'You're so *lucky*!'

Max and Jake slowed down, letting the girls walk on ahead. When they were out of earshot, Jake gave Max a nudge with his elbow.

'So where were you really last week?'

'Up a tree, mostly,' Max shrugged. Jake stared at him, confused. 'I was a cat,' explained Max.

'Yeah right,' snorted Jake. 'Funny how you just happened to change the day the new *Vampire Blasters* game came out. What a coincidence!'

Max stopped. 'What are you saying?' he demanded.

'You can't fool me any more,' said Jake. 'You say you've changed loads of times, so how come I've never seen it?'

'You're just never around when it happens!' Max protested.

'Or maybe it's because you don't change at all!'

'I do so!'

'Prove it then!'

'It doesn't work like that!'

Unnoticed by the boys, an overweight traffic warden strolled up. He tutted quietly as he noted down the number plates of all the cars parked nearby. Every so often he glanced sideways at Max and shuffled a little closer.

If they hadn't been so busy arguing, Max and Jake might have spotted something strange about the warden. They might, for example, have noticed his enormous bushy beard, which almost reached down to his trousers. They might have noticed that his uniform was made up of a dark blue tracksuit and a tiny toy policeman's helmet. If they'd looked really closely they might even have noticed the small, six-legged robot the warden was trying to hide under his notebook.

As it was, they noticed nothing. In fact, they were so busy bickering they didn't even spot the warden slip the robot spy into Jake's backpack.

Sniggering quietly to himself, Professor Preston
Slynk turned on his heel and scampered off,
whistling tunelessly every step of the way.

'Why would I skip school when I knew we had
a big experiment to do?' Max snapped. 'I'm going
to fail the end of term tests now!'

'Well maybe you should have thought of that
before bunking off to play *Vampire Blasters*!'

'I didn't!'

'Right!' Molly snarled, storming over. 'That's enough! You're behaving like a couple of five-year-olds!'

'He started it,' Max mumbled.

'I did not!'

'ENOUGH!' roared Molly. 'I don't care who started it, just stop it!' She glared at Max as he opened his mouth to speak. He quickly thought better of it. 'We're in good time,' she told her brother. 'So we can go into the lab and go through the experiment.'

'Yeah, all right,' Max nodded. 'Thanks.'

'Count me out,' Jake sniffed. 'I'm going to the computer room.' He stalked off, closely followed by Samreen.

'I'll come with you,' she said. 'I need to type up my homework from last night.'

'Right then,' said Molly to Max. 'It's catch-up time!'

A frog was already pinned to the dissection board when Max and Molly slipped into the biology lab. Molly couldn't bring herself to look.

'Is it dead?' she winced.

'Well,' said Max, 'it's got a pin through its head so at a guess I'd say yes.'

'Poor thing,' Molly sighed. 'Still, at least it died in the name of science.'

'And in the name of having its guts squirted across a classroom,' Max reminded her. He grinned at the horrified expression on his sister's face.

'You're sick!' she scowled. 'Now get us some beakers and a test tube while I get my notes out.'

Max saluted and set about collecting the things Molly had asked him to get. While she waited for Max to gather the stuff together she carefully took out the carved mask and looked at it, admiringly.

'It's amazing to think this has come all the way from Africa, isn't it?' she said.

Max glanced over at her, then stopped in his tracks. His face went pale.

'It's not the only thing that's come all the way from Africa,' he gulped. 'Turn it around.'

Molly turned the mask, then let out a piercing scream. The wooden carving slipped from her hands and hit the ground with a clatter. She leapt back just in time to see eight long, hairy legs scurry down from the mask and on to the classroom floor.

'That's a big spider,' Max whistled, not daring to get too close.

'It's a tarantula,' Molly shuddered. 'It must've been in the box from Mum and Dad!'

Max remembered the movement he'd seen in the mask earlier. He opened his mouth to tell Molly about it, but his tongue suddenly felt five sizes too big and all he could manage was a mumble.

'Are you OK?' asked Molly. 'You're all sweaty.'

Max shook his head and clutched his sides. They were aching sharply, like they were about to split wide open!

His skin itched, as thick wiry hairs began to push through his pores. Four big bumps bulged out from his ribs, doubling him over in pain. They stretched and grew until they were as long as his arms.

'M-Molly,' Max managed. He looked up and saw he was less than half the height of his sister. 'I can't miss this lesson!'

Molly watched in amazement as six extra eyes sprouted on her brother's forehead. They blinked at her, one after the other.

Molly had never seen Max transform before and she'd never thought about how painful it must be for him. But there was nothing she could do to help him now. She could only stand and stare as

he shrank before her very eyes.

'P-please,' Max stammered, 'don't let me miss the lesson!'

'Of course I won't,' she nodded. She didn't know what else to say. By the time the words had left her mouth her brother had disappeared beneath a crumpled school uniform on the floor.

Max staggered as he struggled to get the hang of his six extra legs. Slowly he began to make his way along one of his trouser legs. It stretched out before him like a long, dark tunnel.

Well, he thought. *Isn't this just great?*

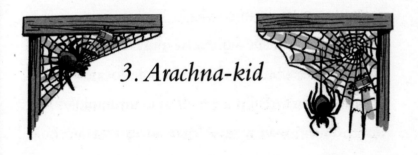

3. Arachna-kid

Molly peeked under the desks, hunting for the real tarantula. In her hands she could feel Max's hairy feet tickle against her skin. It would have made her giggle had she not been busy panicking.

'Come on,' Molly muttered, scanning the classroom for the runaway spider. 'Where are you?'

Clutched between his sister's hands, Max couldn't help but bounce about. He hadn't been thrown around so much since Molly dragged him on the rollercoaster at the fair last year, and he was beginning to feel quite sick.

'I can't see it,' she sighed. 'It must've climbed into a crack somewhere. It should be safe for now.'

Max didn't really care. If the tarantula could travel all the way from Africa on its own it could survive a few hours in a school. He had more important things to think about. Namely a biology lesson he couldn't afford to miss.

'You'll be OK here,' Molly told him. She gently set him down on the floor by her seat. Max looked up and saw eight giant versions of his sister grinning back. He'd probably have nightmares about that sight for the rest of his life. For now, though, he was just glad he'd be able to listen to the lesson, even if he couldn't take part.

The classroom door was suddenly thrown open. It swung hard and smacked against the wall. To Max's ears it sounded like a bomb had just gone off.

'Let's get slicing and dicing!' cackled Stewart Staines, as he strode into the room with the rest of the class close behind. 'Those little froggies won't know what's hit them!'

'Or won't know what's *slit* them,' added Small Paul, Stewart's sidekick, sniggering at his own joke.

'Shut up,' Stewart growled. 'I make the jokes, not you.'

Down on the floor Max felt the sharp hairs on his body rise up. Stewart Staines – or Brain Strain as Max liked to call him – loved to see people suffer. It was no surprise he was so excited about today's dissection.

A toad cutting up a frog, thought Max. *Whatever next?*

Children continued to pour into the classroom, and it suddenly struck Max that he was standing in their path! Concentrating hard on which foot went where he managed to scurry up the leg of Molly's chair. Half a second later, Brain Strain's dirty black boot thudded down right where he'd just been.

'Where's Max?' asked Jake, as he slipped into the seat next to Molly. Around them, the rest of the class chattered excitedly about the dissection.

'He's ... um ... under my chair,' Molly whispered.

Jake leaned back and looked long and hard at her. He glanced down under the seat, then back up at Molly.

'No, he isn't.'

'He is,' Molly insisted. She looked round to make sure nobody was listening in. 'He's changed into a spider!'

'A spider?' asked Jake, flatly.

'A tarantula!'

'Nice try,' Jake shrugged, 'but there's nothing there.'

'There is so,' protested Molly. She leaned to the side and peered under her seat. 'He's just ... Oh, no!'

she gasped. 'Where is he?'

'Last level of *Vampire Blasters*, probably,' sniffed Jake. 'No wonder he keeps beating my score.'

'Max,' Molly hissed, 'where are you?'

At that moment Max was hanging upside down from his sister's chair. Climbing was surprisingly easy – he didn't even have to think about it. He just stuck to whatever he stood on, no matter which way up it was.

'Could you all, er, could we quieten down now, please?' stumbled Miss Burrows as she entered the lab and closed the door gently behind her. The chatter carried on just as loudly as it had before. 'Come on,' she pleaded. 'We've got a lot to get through!'

'Yeah,' sneered Brain Strain. 'Skin, bones and guts for starters!'

Molly rolled her eyes and sat quietly. She liked Miss Burrows and always felt bad for her when the

rest of the class ran riot. It couldn't be easy being a new teacher, especially with Stewart Staines in your class.

'That's right, Stewart,' the teacher nodded. 'But before we start we're going to look at the theory of dissection, and discuss what our reasons are for carrying one out today.'

'To see its brain!' grinned Stewart.

'Yeah, it'll be interesting for you to find out what

one's like,' scowled Molly. 'Since you haven't got one of your own.'

'All right, all right, settle down!' chirped Miss Burrows, trying to stop the fight before it had properly started. 'Now, who wants to tell me some of the reasons we carry out dissections?'

In his hiding place under Molly's seat, Max was struggling to hear what was being said. If he was to have any chance of picking up anything from the lesson he'd have to get closer.

Moving slowly, he crawled down the chair leg and up under Molly's desk. He could hear much better now he was a little nearer the front of the class.

Through a gap between the chairs in front, Max could see Miss Burrows was on the move. He narrowed his eight eyes and tried to stretch to see what she was doing.

'Take a look at this diagram,' she said. She was in

front of the whiteboard, but all Max could see were her legs. 'I'm not saying it'll definitely be in the test, but let's just say it might be worth memorising.'

Max felt a wave of panic washing over him. The teacher given away that the diagram would feature in the end of term test! He had to see it!

He released his grip on the underside of Molly's desk and dropped silently down to the floor. As quickly as he could, he scurried a few rows forwards, weaving between chair legs and past schoolbags which towered above him.

Eventually, he made it to the front row. It took him no time at all to clamber up the leg of the desk and attach himself underneath. The only problem was he still couldn't see the whiteboard properly.

Slowly, he shuffled closer to the front of the desk. Halfway there he felt one leg become trapped. He looked up and winced. His foot was wedged deep into a sticky blob of chewing gum!

Bracing his other legs, Max heaved at the trapped one. The gum stretched into stringy threads as he fought to rescue it. Finally, the leg popped free, and Max felt his grip on the table slipping.

The weight of his body swung him away from the desk, leaving him dangling by two of his legs. He flailed frantically, trying to get a grip on the wood.

He caught hold on the edge of the desk just in time to stop himself falling. He sat there for a moment, not moving, as he got his breath back.

Suddenly, Max heard someone give a sharp gasp. He poked his hairy head round the underside of the table. It was Vicki Veale's desk and Vicki's face was deathly pale and frozen with horror. She pointed a trembling finger down at him.

Max watched helplessly as Vicki opened her mouth to scream. Things were about to get complicated!

4. The Spider Slayer!

Max racked his brains for a way to stop Vicki screaming. His first thought was to spin a big web with the words 'Please Don't Scream' entwined in it, but he quickly realised there wasn't time. *Anyway, do tarantulas even spin webs?* he thought to himself.

He decided to give Vicki a wave. Perhaps then she'd realise he was a friendly spider and she'd forget all about screaming in terror. It wasn't the best idea in the world, but it was the only one he had.

Max lifted one leg and wobbled it around in what he hoped was an unthreatening way.

'WAAAAAAAH!' wailed Vicki. The whole class jumped at the sound of her scream. Max sighed. So much for that plan.

Almost immediately, Brain Strain's face filled Max's field of view.

'What is it?' the bully demanded. The colour drained from his cheeks as he caught sight of Max poking out from under the desk.

'Sp . . . Sp . . .' Staines stammered, his eyes wide and staring.

'What is it, Stewart?' Miss Burrows asked.

'A sp . . . A spi . . .'

Max grinned, baring his venomous fangs. Brain Strain was scared of spiders! Not just scared, either – by the way he was behaving it looked like he was terrified of them. This was way too good an opportunity to miss!

Max scampered up on to the table top and made straight for Brain Strain's hand, which was resting on the desk just a few centimetres away.

Stewart screamed and stumbled backwards; his eyes didn't leave the spider. He scrambled up on to another desk, flailing wildly and sending pens, paper and lab equipment tumbling on to the classroom floor. His boot stamped down on an ink cartridge and a jet of black ink squirted everywhere.

'Oh, no, Max,' sighed Molly, as she realised what

was going on. 'You're such an idiot!'

Out of the corner of three eyes Max spotted a mirror image of himself scurrying away from the falling objects. The other spider weaved left and right, narrowly avoiding a Petri dish, which landed with a crash right behind it.

'Stewart, what are you doing?' demanded Miss Burrows. 'Be careful up there, you might . . .'

Her voice trailed off as she spotted the tarantula on the table. Max turned and looked up at her. Brain Strain was whimpering behind him. Vicki was frozen with horror, her finger still pointing.

Miss Burrows took a deep, steadying breath. When she spoke her voice was soft and quiet.

'Nobody panic, there's nothing to worry about,' she said. 'Everyone slowly move away from the desk. No sudden movements.'

'What is it, Miss?' asked a voice from the back of the class.

'It's nothing to worry about,' the teacher repeated. 'Just a poisonous spider . . .'

The screaming started before Miss Burrows had finished the sentence. Chairs and desks were knocked over as half the class desperately tried to get away from the spider and the other half tried to get closer for a better look.

Max swivelled round and took in the chaos he'd caused. Most of the girls were standing on their chairs at the back of the class, crying. The boys – all except Brain Strain, who was still cowering on the other table – were crowding round the desk, grinning down at him with horrified excitement.

'Don't get too close!' begged Miss Burrows. 'It might bite!'

'What's all the noise in here?' demanded a male voice from the front of the classroom. Everyone turned in time to see Mr Miller striding in, his face like thunder.

'Mr Miller, thank goodness,' sighed Miss Burrows. 'There's a spider on Vicki's desk.'

'A spider,' echoed Mr Miller. 'All this panic for one spider?'

'It . . . it is a *big* spider,' Miss Burrows explained.

'It must be to have scared poor Stewart up on to a desk like that,' grinned Mr Miller. 'You do realise, Mr Staines, that spiders can climb, don't you? They're quite well known for it.'

He looked up at the trembling boy, expectantly. 'I suppose what I'm saying is: get down!' he barked. 'And that goes for the rest of you teetering on your chairs back there. You're here to learn biology, not circus skills.'

Hesitantly, Brain Strain climbed back down from the desk, keeping as much distance between himself and the tarantula as possible. At the back of the class, the girls did the same.

'Now then,' said Mr Miller, 'where's this spider?'

'It's right . . .' began Miss Burrows, turning to Vicki's desk. Max was nowhere in sight. 'It was here a minute ago!' she insisted.

'Well, how do you suggest we deal with it?' asked Mr Miller.

'Stamp on it!' suggested one of the boys.

'No!' shrieked Molly, blushing as everyone turned to look at her. 'I mean . . . that would be cruel.'

'No one is stamping on anything,' insisted Mr Miller. 'We'll catch it alive.'

'Who will?' gasped Miss Burrows. 'I'm not touching it!'

'Come on, Miss Burrows, it's probably more scared of you than you are of it.'

'I doubt that very much!' Miss Burrows scoffed. 'It was the size of a dinner plate. If you're so keen for it to be caught, you do it.'

Mr Miller's smug expression faded just a little.

'I would,' he squirmed, 'but I think we've had

quite enough excitement for one day.' He turned to Brain Strain and clicked his fingers. 'Mr Staines,' he barked, 'as luck would have it we have an exterminator clearing out a wasp's nest from the boys' toilets today. Please go and fetch him and we'll let a professional handle this.'

Stewart nodded and scurried off out of the class, his eyes scanning the floor for creepy crawlies.

'A wasp's nest?' asked Miss Burrows.

'One of the lads from my class found it earlier,' Mr Miller explained. 'The nurse thinks he'll be able to sit down by Thursday.'

Molly ducked down under her desk and searched for signs of Max. She couldn't see him anywhere. There were too many people blocking her view, so she crept slowly closer to Vicki's desk, keeping low and trying not to be noticed.

As she reached the desk, a pair of green paper boots stepped into view. She looked up, past

matching green overalls, until she eventually locked eyes with the tallest man she'd ever seen. His breath wheezed in and out through a white face mask, making him sound like a science-fiction villain.

In one hand he held a spray gun. Every few seconds he'd twirl it on his finger like a cowboy. As it whizzed round and round Molly managed to make out a picture of a spider on the side of the gun. It was flat on its back with its eight legs pulled into its chest.

'This is the Arachna-Eliminator,' drawled the exterminator. 'The most powerful spider-slaying spray gun in the world. It could blow a Black Widow's legs clean off.'

'You're going to kill it?' gasped Molly.

'Well, I got this stuff flown in from America just last week,' said the exterminator. 'And I've been *dying* to put it to the test!'

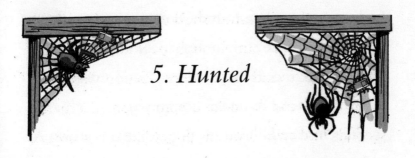

5. Hunted

The exterminator slowly stalked through the classroom, watched closely by Max. He held the spray gun in front of him, sweeping it left and right as he hunted out his prey.

'Here little spider,' he sang. 'Don't be afraid, I won't hurt you.' Behind the mask the exterminator gave a wicked grin. 'Kill you, yes, but not hurt you!'

Max felt all eight of his legs go tense. His body sank even lower to the floor, braced either to fight or flee. At the moment he wasn't sure which to do.

The sensible thing would be to scurry off and find somewhere safe to hide. Something deep down within him wasn't interested in hiding, though. A dark and primal feeling wriggled and struggled as it fought to take him over completely.

He felt scared. Threatened. His instincts screamed at him that the best response to the danger was to bite something. Anything. Whichever poor soul happened to be closest at the time.

But, no! Max was in control, not the spider. No matter how strong the urge was, he wouldn't give in to it. No matter how much the desire overwhelmed him he would resist finding a victim to sink his poison-tipped fangs deep into, piercing their juicy flesh, their warm blood spurting out all over . . .

A sound like thunder shook him from his trance. The children were filing out of the classroom. Their feet thudded noisily on the floor as they stomped by, one after the other.

Max felt his mouth fill with hot saliva as Vicki Veale trudged past in her stylish sandals. His eight beady eyes swivelled and focused on her bare, bony ankle. How easy it would be to scurry over and plunge his teeth right through her bare skin. He raised his body up and began to hurry forwards. Just one little nibble. One teeny bite. Where was the harm in that?

'Aha!' yelled the exterminator. He caught Vicki by the arm and yanked her out of harm's way. 'There you are my little beauty!' he roared.

In one fluid motion, he swung the spray gun down and puffed out a cloud of white powder. It twisted and swirled around Max like a tiny snowstorm. He scampered away as the powder began to sting his eyes.

Blinded, Max staggered and stumbled away from the exterminator. Desperate to escape the stinging cloud of toxic dust, he blundered on, over all obstacles in his path. He slipped and skidded as he crawled through the ink spilled by Brain Strain. His wet feet left tiny black footprints on Molly's fallen exercise book. She'd probably kill him for that, but he didn't have time to worry about it right now.

Behind him he heard chairs and desks being hauled aside as the exterminator hunted him down. Max ran faster, terrified of taking another hit from the Arachna-Eliminator.

He forced open his streaming eyes and scanned the lab for somewhere to hide. The place was a wreck. In their panic, the girls had managed to knock over everything they could possibly have knocked over, but none of the toppled lab equipment offered a decent hiding place.

He could hear the exterminator drawing closer. Any minute now he'd be spraying his powder again. Panicked, Max turned round, scouring the area.

After a few seconds, he spotted a gap between the wall and a damaged floorboard. It would be a tight squeeze, but it looked large enough for him to wedge himself in.

With his eight legs working overtime, Max sped for the crack and squeezed inside. He edged as far into the gap as he could go and sat there silently in the dark, his heart thudding like a drum. All he could do now was wait and see if the exterminator would find him again.

Out in the open, Molly gazed around the classroom along with the few students who had been brave enough to stay and watch the action. All of a sudden, a movement on the floor caught her eye. Something had shot across the floor right next to her. She was certain it was a spider, but which one? Was it Max or was it the real tarantula?

She crouched down, trying to see where the spider had gone. It had been moving pretty fast, but it still couldn't have got far. It had to be somewhere nearby.

'Max,' Molly whispered. 'Max, where are you?'

She paused, listening for an answer, then realised that she wasn't going to get one. Even if Max had heard her, he wasn't in much of a position to reply.

'Can I *please* get some peace and quiet in here?' demanded the exterminator. He was becoming frustrated now, and his trigger finger was getting itchy.

'Yes,' squeaked Miss Burrows. She was holding the door of the lab wide open. 'Let's leave this to the expert. We're just getting in the way here.'

Molly did her best to look like she hadn't heard a word the teacher had said. She dropped to her hands and knees and crawled across the floor, continuing her search for the missing spider. She had to find it before the exterminator did, or Max was going to be in serious trouble.

'Hey, are you looking for it too?' whispered Samreen, as she sidled up to Molly. Her face broke into a wide grin as Molly nodded. 'Let's work together,' she beamed. 'We'll be sure to find it that way!'

'Good idea,' nodded Molly, relieved to have some help. 'Let's get it. Catch it, I mean,' she added in a hurry. 'Let's try and catch it alive.'

'Of course we're going to capture it alive,' grinned Samreen. Her eyes were sparkling in a way

Molly had never seen before, and didn't really like. 'Then we can cut it open instead of the frog!'

'What?!' spluttered Molly. 'You can't do that!'

'Why not?' frowned Samreen.

'Because . . . because . . .' Molly struggled to give a good reason. 'Because it's not nice!'

'Come on, Molly,' Samreen shrugged, 'it's a deadly, disgusting spider we're talking about here, not a cute little kitten. If you ask me, when something like that wanders into a biology class, it's asking to be dissected!'

'Perhaps there's something about "please leave" you girls don't understand?' scowled Mr Miller. Molly and Samreen turned to find him standing behind them. His arms were folded across his chest and he was tapping his foot impatiently.

'Many hands make light work, and all that,' Molly suggested. She smiled, nervously. 'We thought we could help find it.'

'Then you thought wrong,' said the teacher. He stepped towards the girls and placed a hand on each of their backs. Gently but firmly he began to steer them towards the classroom door. 'Now, let's get out of here and let this gentleman do his work.'

Molly tried to come up with an excuse to stay in the room, but she knew, no matter how good a reason she dreamt up, Mr Miller wouldn't listen to it. There was no point in arguing.

Worried, she glanced back over her shoulder. The exterminator idly twirled his spray gun on his finger as his eyes scanned the lab. Standing there with his overalls and mask he looked ruthless – even sinister.

She thought of her brother hiding somewhere in the classroom, all on his own. She thought of the picture of the dead spider on the gun.

'Oh, no,' she whispered. 'He doesn't stand a chance!'

6. Chilling Out

Molly pushed between her classmates, who were all crowded together outside the door of the lab. She squeezed between two girls, ducked under the arm of a taller boy, and finally found who she was looking for.

'Miss Burrows, we've got to stop him killing the spider!' she blurted.

'It's terrible,' the teacher nodded. She was staring into space, wringing her hands together. 'Absolutely terrible.'

'I know!' shrilled Molly. 'That's why we have to stop him!'

'I'll be the laughing stock of the staffroom.'

This caught Molly by surprise.

'Why will you be the laughing stock of the staffroom if he kills the spider?'

'What? No, it's nothing to do with the spider. It's because of all the chaos earlier. No one listened to a word I said. Mr Miller is really going to rub that in at break-time.'

'Who cares?' Molly demanded. 'If we don't get a move on it'll be too late to save the spider!'

'Who cares?' the teacher echoed. 'It's obvious you're not the one who has to put up with the jokes and sarcastic comments! The other teachers will have filled my bag with fake spiders before the break-time bell has finished ringing!'

Molly turned away, leaving Miss Burrows to fret. She stretched up on to her tiptoes and peered over the noisy throng of pupils.

'Jake!' she called. On the other side of the crowd Jake turned at the sound of his name. 'Over here,' Molly shouted, shoving her way through the mass of arms and legs.

'What's up?' asked Jake, as they met somewhere near the middle.

'We've got to get Max out of there,' Molly hissed. 'That guy's going to kill him!'

'Max isn't in there,' Jake scowled. 'I told you I'm not falling for it any more.'

'He is, you've got to believe me!'

'Look, we were together all the way to school,' Jake said, 'but then the moment my back's turned he suddenly . . .' Jake lowered his voice and glanced around to make sure nobody was listening. 'He changes into a spider.'

'Yes, so?'

'So I miss it, like I always do. Don't you think it's strange that I never see him change?'

'So where do you think the spider came from?' asked Molly.

'It was you! You had it in your school bag all along,' said Jake. 'You're not pulling the wool over my eyes any more!'

Molly wanted to argue, but there wasn't enough time. If she was going to rescue her brother she was going to have to do it soon, or there'd be nothing left to save. Her gaze swept over the class, searching for anyone she could count on to help.

Molly's face lit up as she spotted a badge on one girl's blazer. Printed in bright red letters on the badge were the words: *Meat Is Murder.*

'An animal rights activist,' grinned Molly. 'Just what I need!'

'You can't hide forever,' chuckled the exterminator. He was almost bent double, the spray gun held close to the floor. 'I'm a trained expert, you're just a silly little insect.'

Arachnid, you idiot, thought Max. *Even I know a spider's an arachnid, not an insect.*

He felt a powerful urge to run right out there and bite the exterminator on the hand. Then they'd find out who the silly little insect really was!

'So you want to do it the hard way then, do you?' sneered the man in green. He squeezed on the trigger of the gun. Max watched as a puff of poisonous smoke drifted into the air. The exterminator was moving closer with every step. Any minute now Max would be discovered! 'That's OK,' the exterminator continued, 'because between you and me, I much prefer the hard way!'

Max felt his body begin to shiver. He was an African spider and needed African temperatures. He wasn't designed to cope with the cold, and right now he was just a few degrees away from freezing.

He knew the classroom radiator would be hot, but it seemed such a long way away. Even if he ran faster than his eight legs had run before he'd be bound to be spotted. He had to do something, though, or he'd end up a spider-shaped icicle!

He went through his options in his head. He could stay where he was and freeze to death, or make a run for it and be gassed to death. Neither option was very appealing.

Wrapping his legs around his body, Max curled up into a ball and tried to fight off the cold. Out in the classroom the exterminator took another step closer. One way or another Max would have to do something – and fast!

'How will you sleep at night knowing you're responsible for that poor creature's death, Mr Miller?' tutted the girl with the badge.

'Like this,' smiled the teacher. He rested his head on his hands and let out a loud snore.

'Well, I'm glad you think it's funny, sir,' snapped the girl. Molly watched her, impressed at the authority in her voice. 'I'm glad you think killing an innocent creature is a laughing matter.'

Another girl had appeared behind Molly and was looking at the teacher disapprovingly.

'You always tell us bullying's wrong,' she sniffed, 'but that's exactly what you're doing now!'

'It's a poisonous spider!' protested Mr Miller.

'A *rare* poisonous spider,' added Molly. 'My mum and dad sent me some stuff from Africa. I think it stowed away inside.'

Mr Miller looked from one girl to the next. For once he was lost for words. The girls glared at him, until eventually he sighed and shook his head.

'OK, fine,' he shrugged. 'I suppose if it really is rare we should capture it alive.' He clicked his fingers at the nearest pupil, making him jump. 'You boy! Go and ask the receptionist to call the RSPCA.'

'We've got to hurry,' Molly demanded as the boy scurried off to pass on the message. 'For all we know the exterminator's got him . . . I mean *it* . . . already!'

Max pulled his legs tighter around his body and lay shivering in the darkness. He couldn't take this cold much longer. The radiator seemed to call to him, promising him heat. If he were warmer he'd be able to think straight and find a way to escape. Then he could hide out until he changed back.

He uncurled his legs and crept to the entrance of his hidey-hole. The exterminator had his back turned. This was his chance!

Gritting his pointed teeth, Max scurried out of the

crack and sped across the floor. Chair legs whizzed by as he weaved his way across the classroom.

In just a few seconds he was halfway there. The air was already getting warmer the closer he got to the radiator. He was going to make it! He was going to . . .

'Gotcha!' snarled the exterminator.

Max shuffled round to see what was happening. The exterminator was creeping towards him, his finger on the trigger of the Arachna-Eliminator gun.

'You,' cried the man, 'are exterminated!'

7. *Slime for Lunch*

Max stood deathly still as the door to the lab was thrown wide open. Mr Miller burst in, followed by Molly and the other two girls.

'Stop!' Molly shrieked. 'Leave it alone!'

'No chance,' sneered the exterminator. 'I've almost got it!'

'We've decided we won't be needing it killed after all,' explained Mr Miller. 'But thanks all the same.'

'But I almost had it,' whined the exterminator,

his voice cracked and wobbly. 'S'not fair,' he concluded, quietly.

'You've still got those wasps to deal with,' Mr Miller reminded him. 'I doubt anyone will object if you kill them. Right girls?'

'Actually . . .' one of them began.

'Exactly,' beamed Mr Miller, ignoring her. 'No one cares about wasps.'

'All right then,' shrugged the exterminator.

'That's the spirit,' Mr Miller cheered. 'Now off you go and sort that out for us. There's a good man.'

The exterminator hesitated, then turned and stomped from the classroom, dragging his feet behind him every step of the way.

The spider was still standing on the floor in front of Molly. She crouched down and looked into its eight eyes. Six of them were a deep, shiny black, but two shone bright blue. She'd found the right spider!

Molly held out her hand for Max to clamber up,

but something gripped her arm and pulled her away.

'Don't get me wrong,' said Mr Miller, 'I'd like to have the next lesson off just as much as you would, but I don't fancy explaining to the head why I had to rush a girl to hospital with a poisonous spider bite.'

Molly struggled free of the teacher's grasp and turned back to where Max had been. All she could see was a bare patch of floor. Max had disappeared!

Below the radiator, Max basked in the heat, letting it warm him right down to the tips of his legs. Things had got scary for a moment, but he was safe now. He had stopped shivering and was much more comfortable. The only problem was he was now feeling –

Think of something else, he told himself. *Take your mind off it!*

He glanced round and spotted the other spider. It was crouched nearby, warming itself and watching him suspiciously. It had started spinning a web. *So tarantulas do make webs*, thought Max. This one looked a lot more comfortable than he felt. He lifted a leg and gave it a wave. Not surprisingly, it didn't wave back. Max stared at its pointed fangs. They looked perfect for —

No! He closed his eyes tight and tried to fight the desire burning in his belly. It grumbled in complaint, demanding to be filled. The twins' mum and dad had once said that tarantulas could go for weeks without food. A sharp pain shot through Max's abdomen. That definitely wasn't possible for Max-the-tarantula. He had to eat *something*.

He looked around for anything appetising. Maybe someone had dropped a chocolate bar or a packet of crisps. A chocolate bar would be huge now he was small – he could munch on it for hours!

His eyes fell finally on the limp body of the frog, which had been knocked over in the panic. It still dangled from the board it had been pinned to.

No way, thought Max, as his legs began to carry him towards it all on their own. *You can't be serious!*

'Did someone call the RCPSA?' a tubby man chirped as he stepped into the corridor. Mr Miller was leading Molly and the girls out of the class at exactly the same moment.

'Er . . . you mean the RSPCA?' he asked.

'That's what I said!' grinned the man. 'The RSC . . . The animal thing.'

'Yes,' nodded Mr Miller. 'We've got a big spider on the loose.'

'Then I'm your man!' the man beamed.

'I must say you got here quickly,' said Mr Miller. 'We only called a few minutes ago.'

'Yes . . . um . . . well,' the man stumbled. 'I just happened to be in the area, and you know, we at the RPC . . . RSAP . . . Us lot always like to respond as quickly as we can!'

Molly looked closely at the RSPCA man. It took her less than half a second to see through the pathetic disguise.

'Professor Slynk,' she muttered. 'What's he doing at school?'

Max stood over the fallen frog, his front two legs resting on its back. It was almost the same size as him, but slimier and smellier.

Max's jaws opened wide. He wondered how big lumps of frog flesh would feel slipping down his throat; he imagined its slimy skin sliding into his belly. It was enough to make him want to –

His stomach tightened and ejected digestive juices all over the frog. Almost immediately its skin began to turn to a runny goo. Max struggled against the urge to taste the slimy liquid. He tried to back away, but his legs wouldn't let him. The desire was too strong. He couldn't fight it any longer.

Shutting his eyes tight, Max buried his face deep

in the dissolving frog and feasted on its melting flesh!

Molly rummaged in her school bag, hunting for anything that could have been planted by Slynk. She found nothing. How could he have known about Max's transformation?

She glanced over at Jake, who was standing with his back to her. As she watched, a tiny metallic head popped up from inside his bag. It gave a faint 'beep' then disappeared back down into the depths of the satchel once more.

So that was it! Slynk had planted one of his robot spies on Jake. It must have heard her saying Max had changed into the spider. Molly gasped. It was all her fault. If she'd kept her mouth shut Slynk would never have found out! She had to stop him getting into the class.

'Mr Miller,' she said. 'I don't think that's a proper RSPCA man.'

'What makes you say that?' frowned the teacher.

'Yes,' said Professor Slynk, giggling nervously, 'whatever makes you say that?'

Molly scowled at him. She daren't spill the beans or Max's secret could be revealed.

'Well, Molly?' asked Mr Miller.

'I just don't think he's the real thing,' Molly shrugged. 'Don't let him into the lab.'

'One minute you want the spider caught, the next you don't. Make up your mind, girl!' said Mr Miller, sternly.

'If it helps I can show you my ID card,' offered Slynk.

Before the teacher could answer the professor handed over a piece of card with his photo glued to it. On the top left corner of the card the letters

RPSCA had been written in black marker pen.

'"Mr Webb",' read Mr Miller. '"Expert in Exotic Spiders and Stuff".That's quite a title,' he concluded, handing back the fake ID.

'Thank you,' grinned Slynk. 'We ran out of proper cards back at the office,' he explained. 'Waiting on the new one arriving any day now.'

'Good enough for me,' Mr Miller shrugged. 'In you go.'

'What?!' shrieked Molly. 'But you –'

'Molly, that's enough,' snapped Mr Miller. 'Mr Webb is here to do a job. Stand aside and let him do it.'

Reluctantly she stepped to one side. Professor Slynk, with his back to Mr Miller, stuck out his tongue at Molly as he stepped into the classroom and slowly creaked the door closed behind him.

8. Slynk Versus Spider

Max looked up and almost choked on a mouthful of frog. The obviously false moustache, the badly fitting Spider-Man T-shirt – it could only be Slynk in one of his worst disguises yet.

Still, what Slynk lacked in dress sense he more than made up for in wickedness. At least the exterminator only wanted to kill Max. If Slynk caught him he'd keep him alive by whatever means necessary in order to discover the secret of his power.

While Slynk began to search the room, Max

scurried off to find a hiding place. He sighed as he darted into the shadows at the back of the class. Why did life have to be so complicated?

'Hey! Get off!'

'Jake, look!' snapped Molly. She yanked the robot spy from Jake's bag and held it up for him to see. 'We've been spied on! The RSPCA man isn't a man from the RSPCA at all. It's Professor Slynk, and he's here to catch Max!'

Jake took the tiny insect-like robot from her and studied it closely. It beeped softly in his hand.

'*Now* do you believe me?' Molly asked.

Jake hesitated, then handed her the robot back.

'I've seen more convincing-looking robots in the toy shop.'

'OK, fine,' snarled Molly. 'I couldn't care less if

you believe me, but Max is in danger and if you're half the friend you say you are you'll help me save him.'

Jake looked at his feet. His lips moved silently as he figured out what he should do.

'Please, Jake,' said Molly, softly. 'I'm telling the truth. If we don't do something Max is going to die – or worse.'

'Supposing I did believe you,' began Jake, lifting his head, 'what would be the plan?'

Molly grinned. 'First we need to get into the lab,' she said.

Both children turned and looked over at Mr Miller. He was standing directly in front of the door, stopping anyone getting in or out.

'Well, then,' nodded Jake, 'let's get to it!'

Max crouched down in the shadows, his back against the wall. He couldn't retreat any further. There was nowhere left to run.

'Come out, come out wherever you are, Max,' Slynk smirked. He was zig-zagging slowly across the class, making sure he covered every last inch of the floor. 'I've got you this time,' he sang. 'Soon your special abilities will be mine to control!'

Max swallowed hard and began to climb the back wall. If he couldn't run away he'd run *up*. Maybe Slynk wouldn't spot him hiding on the ceiling.

Maybe.

'So you see, we have to get into the class,' gasped Jake. Beside him Molly nodded enthusiastically. 'I've left my bag in there.'

'And I've left my mobile phone on my desk,' added Molly. 'If I don't get it it'll get covered in spider webs. It'll be ruined!'

Mr Miller stared down at the chattering children, his face barely moving.

'My pen!' shrieked Jake. 'I've left my pen in there, too!'

'A pen,' sighed Mr Miller. 'You want to go back in for a pen?'

'It's a very special pen, sir,' insisted Jake. 'My grandad brought it home from the war.'

'Oh really? And which war was this?'

Jake swallowed nervously. History wasn't exactly his strong point.

'The . . . er . . . Hundred Years' War,' he said.

'The Hundred Years' War?' Mr Miller repeated. 'Which ended in 1453?'

'Yep,' nodded Jake, weakly. 'He's dead old my grandad.'

'I really need to get my phone, sir,' interrupted Molly. 'And I've left a biology book in there I'll need for studying.'

'For one, Miss Murphy – as everyone should be fully aware – mobile phones are not permitted in class. I'm surprised to hear you have one, but don't worry, I'll be sure to rectify that when I confiscate it.'

'But –'

'I'm not finished,' Mr Miller snapped. 'Your biology book you can pick up after class. As for you, Mr Ramsbottom,' he sighed, turning to Jake, 'Ignoring your six-hundred-year-old pen, what else did you say you'd left behind?'

'My bag,' said Jake, hopefully.

'This bag?' asked Mr Miller, hooking one finger through the strap over Jake's shoulder and giving his backpack a hard tug.

'Erm . . . y–yes,' stammered Jake.

'In that case, I think we can safely say the crisis is over,' said the teacher. 'Now please step away from the door. No one is getting into this classroom until that spider has been dealt with!'

Molly opened her mouth to speak, but a glare from Mr Miller silenced her. It was no use. Max was on his own!

Halfway up the wall, Max heard Slynk give a cry of triumph. He looked up in time to see the professor charging straight for him. Swiftly lifting his legs he let his body drop to the floor. He hit the ground hard and rolled clumsily under a desk.

The table was thrown aside, revealing a cackling Slynk. He crouched down, his chubby hands reaching out for the stunned spider.

Max quickly uncurled and managed to stagger

away. He scrambled across the floor, over chairs and under desks as he struggled to shake Slynk off.

The professor blundered after him, leaping over some obstacles and crashing into others. Chairs and desks were strewn in his wake as Slynk tried to follow Max's twisting path across the lab.

Max's heart was beating so fast he thought it might explode. No matter how fast he ran, Slynk always seemed to be right behind. It wasn't fair, his legs were tiny. For every fifty steps he took, Slynk only had to take one to catch up!

Suddenly, the tips of Slynk's fat fingers brushed against his back. Max's whole body quivered in disgust at the faint touch. Behind him, he heard the professor muttering and cursing as some sharp tarantula's hairs stuck like pins into his fingertips.

Max didn't dare laugh at Slynk's discomfort. If he was lucky it might buy him some breathing space, but he knew there was no way a few barbed hairs would stop the professor's pursuit.

Sure enough, he could already hear Slynk closing the gap. Pushing himself hard Max sped across to a large metal cabinet which stood against the lab wall. Slynk's footsteps pounded steadily closer as Max ran. This was going to be close!

With his chest heaving, Max made it to the cabinet just in the nick of time and scampered underneath. He heard a deafening 'crash' as Slynk smacked straight into the side of it. The force of the collision left an almost perfect imprint of the professor's face in the shiny stainless steel.

Rocked by the blow, the cabinet began to topple over. Max darted out from under it. A huge shadow passed across him as Slynk tumbled to the floor, and Max had to roll sideways to avoid being crushed by the professor's blubbery frame.

Suddenly, something smashed on the floor right next to Max's head, spraying him with foul-smelling

water and fragments of razor-sharp glass. He looked up and gasped in horror.

The cabinet was filled with row after row of pickled animals in jars. Now that it was leaning away from the wall, the jars were slipping out!

Max watched helplessly as a second jar slid out. It fell like a fat, deadly raindrop. Max's body tensed as a terrible realisation hit him.

He was directly in its path!

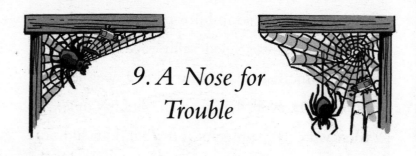

9. A Nose for Trouble

With a yelp of triumph, Slynk launched himself at Max. Just as the professor's podgy hands snatched at the spider, the falling jar smashed hard across the back of his balding head. It shattered into a hundred pieces, stunning him and showering him with a mix of pickling preservative and broken glass.

Max giggled to himself and scurried away, leaving Slynk face down in a puddle on the floor. Slynk groaned quietly, and carefully felt his aching

skull. He shrieked with horror as his fingers found the pickled remains of a baby shark nestling in his hair.

Thanks, shark, thought Max. *You just saved my life!*

Halfway across the classroom the other spider was fleeing from all the noise. It darted left and right as it searched for a safe place to hide. Max understood exactly how it felt. The poor thing was a long way from home. It must have been scared stiff.

It definitely had the right idea, though. The only way Max was going to survive to the end of the lesson was by finding somewhere to hide. But where? Picking out a good hiding place should be easy when you're only a few centimetres long but, despite his best efforts, Max was finding it very difficult to come across one.

He crawled over the lino floor of the lab as quickly as he could, his eight eyes swivelling as he sought out somewhere to shelter from Slynk. The blow he'd taken from the falling glass jar would slow Slynk down, but it wouldn't stop him. Max knew the professor well enough to know *nothing* would stop him if he thought there was a chance of finding out how the transformations worked.

As if on cue, Max heard Slynk pull himself forwards, crying sharply as he dragged himself through shards of broken glass. For someone who claimed to have so many fancy qualifications, he really could be an idiot sometimes!

Slynk advanced slowly, crawling on his belly so as to be at the same level as Max. His clothes were soaked through with pickling solution. His hair was dotted with bits of shark. His stomach and legs were getting more and more scratched by the second. He didn't care. This time he was going to catch the boy. This time he was going to succeed. He could feel it!

'A spider's-eye view to catch a spider,' Slynk

leered. He crept below a desk, his chin nearly touching the ground. It almost looked like he was sniffing the air and letting his nose lead him to his prey. 'You can't run forever, Max,' he said. 'Before today is over I'll be dissecting you like a frog! That's a promise.'

Max felt panic grip him as he reached the corner of the classroom without finding a single safe place to hide. Slynk was creeping closer. Max felt like he should run, but his spider instincts forced him to freeze. If he could stay absolutely still Slynk might not notice him. Maybe he could remain motionless long enough for the change to wear off. Slynk might get away with carrying a spider out of the class, but he'd find it more difficult to get past Mr Miller with a struggling boy over his shoulder.

From down on the floor, Slynk had already locked the spider in his sights. Carefully, the professor reached into his pocket and pulled out a soggy piece of cardboard. Without taking his eyes off the spider, that stood like a statue in the corner of the room, he folded the card into the shape of a small box and grinned a beastly grin. This would be almost too easy!

Outside in the corridor Molly let out a sharp gasp. She'd been watching events through the small window in the biology lab door, and could see that Slynk was about to get his hands on her brother!

'Mr Miller!' she cried. 'You've got to let me in!'

'How many times do I have to tell you?' the teacher snapped. 'Nobody is getting into this classroom until that spider is caught.'

'But –'

'No buts, Miss Murphy,' he scolded. 'Or it'll be straight to the head's office. Understood?'

Molly turned away and pressed her face back up to the glass. Slynk glanced over and flashed a nasty smile in her direction. He mimed catching the spider and squishing it between his hands. Molly felt her blood boil. Slynk would pay for this!

Helplessly, she watched as the professor crawled closer to the spider. His nose was just a few millimetres away from it now. No matter how fast the tarantula might run it wasn't going to get out of grabbing distance in time. Slynk slipped open the lid of the box and prepared to pounce.

'Come on, Max,' Molly whispered, urging the stationary spider to move. 'Get away from there before it's . . .'

Too late! Giggling with delight, Slynk thrust out a hand and clamped it down over the top of the tarantula, trapping it against the floor.

'N-no!' stammered Molly. Tears stung the corners of her eyes. 'He can't have caught him. He can't!'

Slynk carefully made a slight gap in his fingers so he could peer inside and see his captive close up. He edged closer to get a better look at his eight-legged prisoner. His fake moustache wobbled and almost fell off as his face broke into a wide, beaming smile.

'Well, I'd like to say it's been fun, but I'd be lying,' Slynk smirked. 'Just so you understand exactly what's going on, I'm going to put it in language you understand,' he continued. 'Game Over!'

Suddenly there was a flurry of motion in Slynk's hands. The professor squealed as two sharp fangs shot through the gap in his fingers and sank deep into the tip of his nose.

'Yes!' cheered Molly outside the class. She watched Slynk leap to his feet and stagger backwards, frantically trying to rub his aching nose on his sleeve. Molly knew that tarantula bites aren't usually fatal to humans, but there was no doubting the fact that getting one on the end of the nose

would definitely hurt. Judging by the way Slynk was hopping from foot to foot and crying, the bite didn't just hurt a bit – it hurt *a lot*!

Despite the fact that his nose was turning red and beginning to swell up, Slynk somehow managed to keep hold of the spider. Half blinded by tears, the professor fumbled his hand inside the cardboard box, then quickly folded the top shut. Growling, he gave the box a hard shake. Even through the glass of the door Molly could hear the contents thudding around helplessly inside.

'Dare to bite me, will you?' hissed Slynk. 'Just you wait. I had planned to keep the pain to a minimum as I cut you up, but now I'm going to take my time and make sure you feel every single last slice of the blade!' He gave the box another rattle and peered through a gap in the lid at the stunned spider inside. 'You'll pay for that,' he crowed. 'You'll pay dearly!'

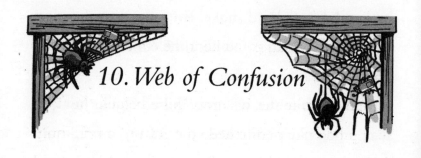

10. Web of Confusion

Tucked away in the corner of the room, Max watched the scene playing out before him. It was a huge relief that Slynk had caught the wrong spider, but even so he felt bad that it was going to get dissected in his place.

Still, it was impossible not to be amused by Slynk's celebrations. He was bouncing around like an excited puppy and punching the air, all the while grinning like an idiot. Every so often, he'd jump up and try to click his heels together. So far, he'd tried the move three times, and each time he'd almost broken his legs.

Max felt a laugh building in his belly as Slynk skipped like a ballet dancer over to the exit, the box tucked safely under his arm. As he neared the door the professor performed a clumsy twirl, only stopping when his swollen nose smacked hard against the classroom wall.

Slynk staggered for a few moments as he regained his balance. When the world had stopped spinning he yanked open the classroom door and pushed his way out into the corridor.

As he watched Slynk disappear through the door, Max felt his laugh bubble up and burst from his throat. He was stunned to hear it echo around the empty classroom.

With a *thud* his head hit against the underside of the desk he was hiding beneath. He looked down and realised he was no longer a spider. Instead he was his normal human self, sitting naked in the corner of the lab. He laughed louder still, relieved to have made it through the lesson in one piece.

'Now then,' he mumbled, as it suddenly dawned on him that he was completely naked. 'Where's Molly hidden my clothes this time?'

Out in the corridor Professor Slynk sidled his way past the pupils, holding the box before him like the Olympic torch. Mr Miller stood firmly in front of Molly, blocking her way.

'Are you OK, Mr Webb?' the teacher frowned. Slynk's whole face had begun to bulge outwards, and his head now resembled a huge, purple balloon. 'You look a bit . . . puffy.'

Slynk moved his head slowly up and down like a nodding dog. He attempted a smile, but his lips were so swollen it was impossible to make it out.

Just as the professor reached the double doors that led out of the corridor, they were thrown wide open. He screamed as one of them crashed straight into his face, knocking him to the ground. A large shadow suddenly loomed over him.

'H-hello,' stammered Miss Burrows as she approached a uniformed man standing in the doorway. 'Can I help you?'

'Thanks for the offer, ma'am, but *I'm* here to help *you*,' smiled the man. He politely lifted his peaked cap, revealing a head of neatly cropped hair. 'Rick Steed,' he beamed, holding up an official-looking ID card. 'RSPCA.'

'What?' frowned Miss Burrows. 'But I thought . . .' Her voice trailed off as she looked down at Slynk, who was now cowering on the floor.

'See!' cried Molly in triumph. 'I *told* you he wasn't really from the RSPCA!'

'Yes, thank you, Molly,' tutted Mr Miller. He strode over to the genuine officer and studied his identification card.

'We got a call a short while ago saying you had a non-domestic arachnid on the premises,' explained the man from the RSPCA. 'Would have been here sooner but there was an incident with a mongoose on the other side of town.'

'We thought *this* man had been sent to sort things out,' Mr Miller said, nodding in Slynk's direction. 'He said he was from the RSPCA.'

'Impersonating an officer, eh?' glowered the uniformed man. 'The Society doesn't look kindly on that sort of thing.' Slynk seemed to shrink as the officer gave him an angry glare.

'Who are you?' the man demanded. 'What have you done with the spider?' He studied the professor's face more closely. 'And why does your head look like a purple potato?'

Slynk tried to reply, but all his bloated lips and swollen tongue could manage was a weak mumble.

'Speak up, man! Where's the spider?'

'The box,' cried Jake. 'He's got it in the box!'

The RSPCA man held out a hand. Slynk shook his bulging head and pulled the box in close against his chest.

'Come on, you're only making things worse.'

'What's going on?' asked Max as he hopped from the biology lab, pulling on one of his shoes.

'Max!' gasped Molly.

'Max Murphy!' snapped Mr Miller.

'Mmpfhm!' wailed Slynk.

'Give me the box,' the RSPCA man demanded, still staring at Slynk. 'Your head's twice the size it should be, man! Give me the spider and I'll take you to hospital!'

Realising that the box was absolutely worthless to him, Slynk quickly handed it over. He didn't know how he'd ended up catching the wrong spider, and right now he was in too much pain to figure it all out. There'd be other chances to catch the boy and learn his secrets. *This battle might be over,* he thought, *but the war will continue until Max's power is mine to command!*

Groaning quietly, and barely able to see past his swollen eyelids, Slynk got shakily to his feet and let himself be led out of the school and off to hospital.

Further along the corridor Miss Burrows was on the warpath.

'I thought everyone had been told to get out of the classroom!' she snapped. Max flashed her his best innocent smile, but she paid it no attention.

'You deliberately went against a direct instruction. I'm fed up with everyone thinking they can ignore what I say just because I'm new!' The teacher's face was red with anger now. The children were silent. No one had ever seen her like this.

'So at lunchtime you're going to find yourself in detention, and I'm going to make you redo last week's experiment. How do you like that?'

Max fought back a grin. If he did that experiment there was a chance he could pass the end of term tests. Miss Burrows' punishment was the best present he could have hoped for.

'Oh, well,' he sighed, winking at Molly, 'I guess that'll teach me a lesson.'

'And you're not the only one,' said Mr Miller. 'Jake and Molly were both very keen to get back into the class, so they can join you tomorrow. Besides, I expected more from you, Miss Murphy,' he said, holding up Molly's biology notes. 'Look at the state of your work.' The twins and Jake studied the tiny inky footprints leading across the page. 'It looks like a spider's crawled across it!'

The children glanced at each other and grinned as the teachers moved off and tried to restore order

to the corridor. After the events of the last hour a lunchtime of detention would be a welcome break.

'A spider, eh?' asked Jake.

'Yep,' nodded Max.

'And I missed the change again.'

'Yep,' repeated Max, bracing himself for an argument.

'Well, then,' Jake smiled. 'I guess we've got all lunchtime for you to tell me about it!'

Max grinned. It was good to have his friend back.

'Count on it,' he said, and the three of them walked off along the corridor side by side.

More Superb Spider Facts!

They're dangerous!
Black widow spiders are among the nastiest of all *arachnids* (from the Greek word meaning spider). Not only do the females sometimes kill and eat their mate, but their bite can also be fatal to humans. Yikes!

They work up an appetite!
Not all spiders use webs to catch their dinner. The wolf spider prefers to chase its prey.

They really work up an appetite!
Female spiders have been known to live on nothing but water for over two years!

They're helpful!
A house spider eats as many as 2,000 insects a year, so remember who to call when you have a fly buzzing around your room!

They're shy!
A spider can hide by using its colours and patterns for camouflage to blend in with its environmnent.

They're sharp shooters!
As well as their nasty bite, tarantulas can launch tiny hairs from their bodies, which can stick into predators and scare them off!

ONLY JOKING!

What do you do to make a spider angry?

Drive him up the wall!

What do you get if you cross a tarantula with a rose?

I'm not sure, but I wouldn't try smelling it!

What do you call 100 spiders on a tyre?

A spinning wheel!

Are you as crawly as the creepie

1. Your science teacher looks a little fed up. Do you:

A Give them the apple from your lunchbox to cheer them up

B Give them a friendly smile as you leave class

C Give them some serious competition: if anyone can do fed up, you can

2. A boy in your class is having a party. You want to go but haven't been invited. Do you:

A Buy him an early birthday present

B Make an effort to be a bit more friendly

C Accept that you won't be going to the party

3. Your mum's had a dreadful new haircut and now she's too embarrassed to take you to the fair. Do you:

A Tell her it's the best haircut she's ever had and that it makes her look really young and pretty! (There's no way you're not going to the fair!)

B Find her a hat to wear

C Settle down for an afternoon of TV watching

4. Your dad's got a cash bonus at work and you'd like him to share the wealth. Do you:

A Fetch his slippers, make him a cup of tea and look enthralled when he tells you all about his fascinating day at the office

B Ask him for more pocket money

C Nothing – there's no way you could part a meanie like him from his cash!

5. Have you done any of the following in the past month?:

- Paid a compliment when you haven't really meant it?
- Laughed at a joke that just wasn't funny for fear of a particular group or person thinking you're un-cool
- Bought someone a present in the hope that they'd like you more
- Snitched on a mate to get in with someone else
- Believed that being popular is more important than pretty much anything else
- Fibbed to a friend because you wanted something from them

SCORING

Score 2 points for every A, 1 point for every B and no points for every C. For question 5, score 1 point for each thing you did.

CONCLUSIONS

10–14 You're such an expert crawler, you make a spider look second best! You'd do pretty much anything to get people to react to you in the way you want. On the other hand, you may just be super-nice, really generous and hugely popular. You decide!

5–9 You're a down-to-earth person and aren't too bothered what other people think of you. You wouldn't go out of your way to suck up to someone just to get them to like you, but you would help a friend in need in order to keep them happy.

0–4 You're not a creepy crawler. You're just not very interested in going out of your way to get what you want. If it seemed like you were after something, you'd take the present back to the shop, eat the chocolate bar and keep the compliments to yourself.

UNCLE HERBERT'S SPIDER-WEB DIP

Here's how to make salsa more exciting *without* adding custard to it like Uncle Herbert always does . . .

YOU'LL NEED:

A big bag of tortilla chips or crisps

A jar of salsa

A tub of guacamole

A small carton of sour cream

A small sealable sandwich bag

A grown-up helper

HERE'S WHAT TO DO:

1. Put the guacamole into a bowl and tip the salsa on top, shake the bowl lightly to even the surface

2. Next, get a small sealable sandwich bag and cut a very tiny hole in one corner

4. Pour the sour cream into the bag and seal the sealable end

5. Squidge the cream over the dip in a spiral

6. Using a butter knife, draw some lines from the centre of the dip to the outer edges of the dish to create a 'web' pattern (see photo)

7. Serve with tortilla chips

YUM!

1. Madagascan Misery

'How many times do you think I can get this to skip?' asked Molly, as she held up a smooth, flat stone.

'Dunno,' shrugged Max. 'Once?'

'Once?!' his twin sister shrilled. 'I could do it once in my sleep!'

Max leant back on the rock he was sitting on and squinted in the midday sun. He shuffled a little to the left so Molly's shadow blocked out the glare.

'Twice then,' he sighed.

'Ten times – easy,' Molly crowed, as she turned to face the vast, motionless lake which lay before them. 'Or I'll be your slave for the day.'

'I'm not being *your* slave if you do it though,' Max quickly insisted.

'That's OK,' his sister shrugged, 'you're more or less my slave anyway.'

Molly closed one eye, held her breath, and flicked the stone out over the water. It skimmed the surface a dozen times before sinking below the brilliant blue surface.

'Twelve times!' she beamed.

'You must be very proud,' said Max, sarcastically.

'Now then,' Molly began, 'how many times do you think I can skip *this* one?'

Max placed his hands behind his head and lay back on the rock. He closed his eyes and did his best to block out Molly's chattering. Even with his eyes closed he could still see the bright orange tones of the blazing sun.

Of all the terrible trips their parents had brought them on, this was one of the worst. He knew, of course, that his mum and dad wouldn't go anywhere if there weren't a wide range of animals to study, but he hadn't expected Madagascar to be quite so full of the things.

On their first day on the island their dad had told them that five per cent of the world's animal species could be found in Madagascar. By the end of the fourth day Max felt like he'd changed into almost all of them. At the last count he'd been a longhorn beetle, a praying mantis, a fork-crowned lemur and a tomato frog. Apart from the praying mantis, he'd never even heard of any of them before this trip! His transformations often turned into really exciting adventures, but with so many changes – well, it was just too much.

'You'd better not fall asleep, you'll get sunstroke,' Molly warned him.

'I'm tired,' Max groaned. 'It's not easy changing every few hours!'

'*You're* tired?' his sister snapped. 'I'm the one who has to trudge around trying to find you whenever you transform. Have you any idea how hard it is to find one little red frog in a rainforest?'

'Have you any idea how hard it is to *be* one little red frog in a rainforest?' Max replied. He sat up on the rock and shielded his eyes with his hand. 'There are things in there that eat little red frogs for breakfast.' Just then his stomach gave a loud rumble. 'Speaking of which, it's lunchtime.'

'Do you ever think about anything apart from food?'

'Course,' sniffed Max, as he got to his feet and dusted himself down. 'If I'm not hungry I don't think about food at all.'

'Oh, yeah? And when are you not hungry?'

'Never!' Max grinned.

The twins walked slowly towards their hotel, dragging their feet behind them. Neither one was looking forward to another encounter with their parents, who had been cross with them for almost the entire trip.

'You think Mum and Dad are still annoyed?' Max asked.

'Probably,' Molly replied. 'They still think we've spent the week sleeping and hanging around the hotel. I bet they had lots of educational day trips planned for us.'

'You know, when you put it like that,' said Max, 'being chased by hungry snakes yesterday suddenly doesn't seem quite so bad.'

'D'you think we should tell them the truth?'

Max stopped and stared at his sister.

'Are you crazy?' he gasped. 'I thought we agreed never to tell them?'

'I know, I just thought it might make life easier,' Molly suggested. 'Instead of having to hide things all the time.'

'I wouldn't be able to hide anything even if I wanted to. They wouldn't let me out of their sight! They'd have a book written all about me in a week, and I could wave goodbye to any chance of a normal life!'

Molly shrugged as they started walking again.
'Yeah, I suppose.'

'So we keep it to ourselves, right?'

'Right,' Molly nodded.

They shuffled on in silence for a few minutes, each lost in their own thoughts.

'D'you think anyone's found those jewels yet?' asked Molly, eventually.

'Which jewels?'

'The stolen jewels,' said Molly. Max looked at her, his face blank. 'The ones I've told you about four times now.' She sighed and shook her head. 'Do you ever listen to anything I say?'

'Sorry, did you say something?' smirked Max. 'I wasn't listening.'

Molly growled and punched her brother hard on the arm.

'There was a big shipment of diamonds and stuff being taken from Kuala Lumpur to Zambia for some prince or other,' she explained for the fifth time. 'It went missing when it was passing through here. I told you all this!'

'No, you didn't,' Max protested.

'I did too! *Four* times! Last time you said "Ooh, that's interesting" and then started talking about food.'

'Did I?' frowned Max. 'Interesting.' He lifted his nose in the air and smiled broadly. 'Now come on, I smell lunch!'

As the twins entered the hotel, Molly held up a hand for Max to stop. She put her finger to her lips and nodded in the direction of the hotel reception. Max looked over and felt his heart leap into his throat.

'Professor Sly-ink,' smiled the receptionist,

reading the name from the reservations book.

The overweight man in front of her mopped his sweaty brow with a spotty handkerchief and scowled. With his other hand he swatted wildly at the flies that buzzed around him.

'Slynk,' he corrected. 'Professor Preston Slynk.'

'Sly-ink,' said the receptionist, uncertainly.

'No, not Sly-ink. *Slynk.*'

'Ah! Slynk. Like stink?'

'Yes,' Slynk sighed. 'That's me.'

Molly let out a giggle and the twins had to duck behind a statue to avoid being seen by the professor.

'What's he doing here?' hissed Max, quietly.

'Mum said he might be coming,' Molly whispered.

'Why didn't you tell me?'

'I did!'

'Oh,' said Max. 'Well, why's he here?'

'Something to do with a night-vision telescope for watching lemurs,' Molly told him.

'I bet that's not the real reason,' said Max, grimly. 'He'll be after me the first chance he gets.'

'Maybe not,' Molly shrugged. 'Maybe he's really just here to help build the telescope. Or maybe,' she grinned, 'he's the one who stole the jewels and he's hanging around until he can get them out of the country.'

'Yeah,' Max laughed. 'He'll have used his little robot spies to do all the dirty work. No security system in the world could hope to stand in the way of Professor Preston Slynk, the greatest criminal mind of our time!'

'Maybe that's why his belly's so big,' added Molly. 'That's where he keeps all the stuff he steals!'

The twins fell about laughing, trying unsuccessfully to imagine Slynk as an international jewel thief.

'Maybe we should tell the police,' suggested Molly. 'It would be nice to see him slung into an African jail.'

'It would,' nodded Max, smiling at the thought. 'And I'd happily be the one to throw away the key!'